GF
GF

D0351921

HULK ™

THE MOVIE STORYBOOK

UNIVERSAL PICTURES PRESENTS IN ASSOCIATION WITH MARVEL ENTERPRISES A VALHALLA MOTION PICTURES / GOOD MACHINE PRODUCTION AN ANG LEE FILM "THE HULK"
ERIC BANA JENNIFER CONNELLY SAM ELLIOTT JOSH LUCAS AND NICK NOLTE MUSIC BY MYCHAEL DANNA COSTUME DESIGNER MARIT ALLEN EDITOR TIM SQUYRES A.C.E. PRODUCTION DESIGNER RICK HEINRICHS
DIRECTOR OF PHOTOGRAPHY FREDERICK ELMES A.S.C. EXECUTIVE PRODUCERS STAN LEE KEVIN FEIGE PRODUCED BY GALE ANNE HURD AVI ARAD JAMES SCHAMUS LARRY FRANCO WRITTEN BY JAMES SCHAMUS DIRECTED BY ANG LEE

MARVEL THIS FILM IS NOT YET RATED   SPECIAL VISUAL EFFECTS AND ANIMATION BY INDUSTRIAL LIGHT & MAGIC   www.thehulk.com   A UNIVERSAL PICTURE UNIVERSAL
THE HULK AND RELATED COMIC BOOK CHARACTERS ™ & © 2003 MARVEL CHARACTERS, INC.   © 2003 UNIVERSAL STUDIOS

The Hulk™: The Movie Storybook

First published in the USA by HarperCollins Publishers Inc. in 2003
First published in Great Britain by HarperCollinsEntertainment in 2003

HarperCollinsEntertainment is an imprint of HarperCollinsPublishers Ltd,
77 - 85 Fulham Palace Road, Hammersmith, London W6 8JB

The HarperCollins website address is
www.fireandwater.com

1 3 5 7 9 10 8 6 4 2

ISBN 0-00-716243-X

Printed and bound in Great Britain by Scotprint

www.thehulk.com

HULK™

THE MOVIE STORYBOOK

Adapted by Laura Driscoll

Based on the motion picture screenplay

written by James Schamus

HarperCollins*Entertainment*

An Imprint of HarperCollins*Publishers*

Inside their lab near San Francisco, scientists Bruce Banner and Betty Ross were testing molecular robots called nanomeds.

A frog was placed inside a machine called the gammasphere. They released a gas containing the nanomeds, which the frog inhaled. Then they shot the frog with gamma rays, piercing its skin.

Inside the frog's body, the nanomeds healed the wound! The only trace left was a bright green scar where the cut had been.

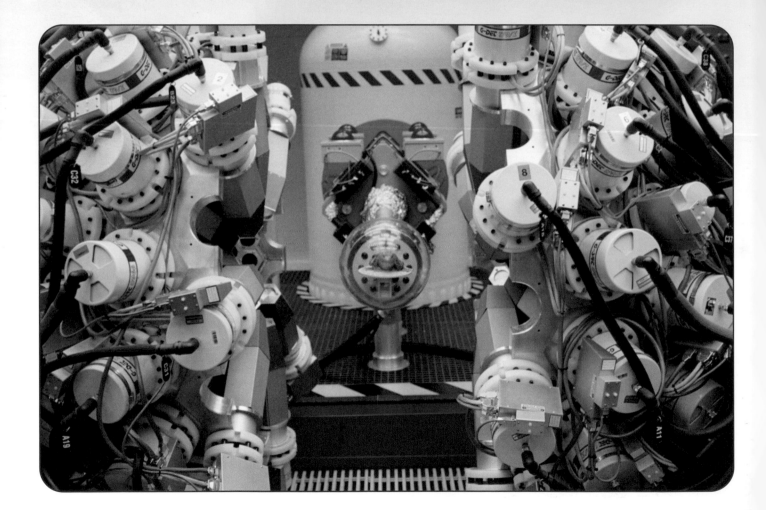

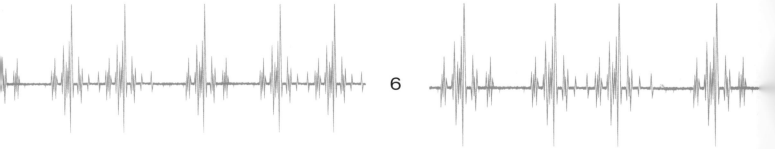

   The nanomeds also released a tremendous amount of energy. It was too much for the frog's body to take and . . . *splat!* Not one frog had survived the experiment.

   Still, if nanomeds could be made safe for humans, they could help keep people healthy. Bruce and Betty knew they were on to something.

So did Glen Talbot. He worked with Betty's father, General "Thunderbolt" Ross, and headed a lab called Atheon.

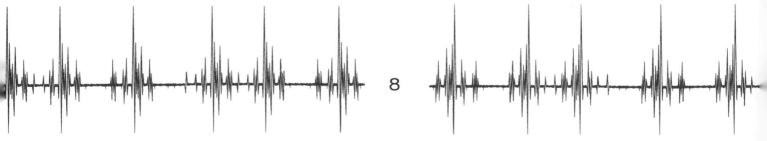

Talbot was interested in Bruce and Betty's work—and in Betty. But Betty only cared for Bruce, even if he was hard to get to know.

Bruce wasn't so sure he knew himself. He had been adopted as a child, but he had no memories of his early childhood.

At night, Bruce had trouble sleeping. He woke up from nightmares he couldn't remember.

And lately, he had the feeling that he was being watched. Who was that strange man outside his window?

One day, there was an accident in the lab. Instead of the frog, *Bruce* inhaled the nanomeds . . . and was blasted with gamma radiation!

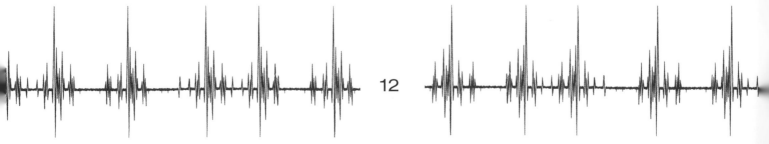

Bruce should have died . . . either from the radiation or from the nanomeds.

Amazingly, the doctor in the lab's infirmary couldn't find anything wrong with him.
That night, Bruce had a visitor.
"You're wondering why you're still alive, aren't you?" the man said. "You're thinking: there's something inside, something different. I can help you understand, if you'll let me."

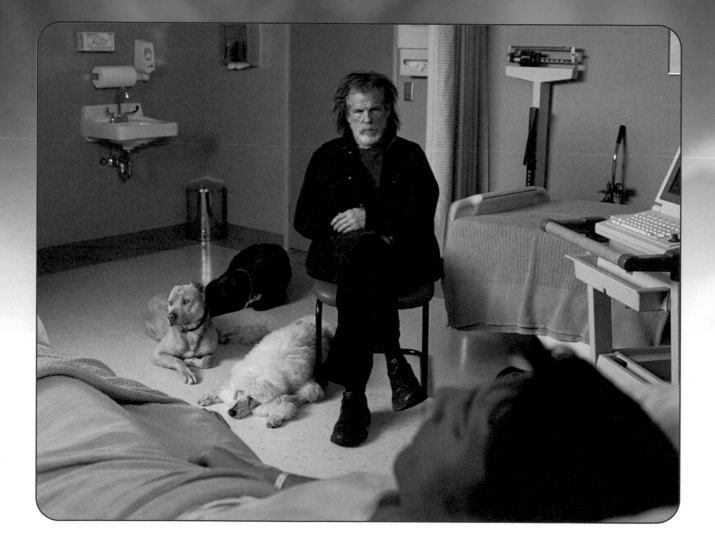

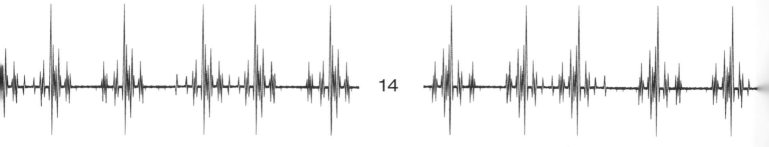

The man said he was David Banner, Bruce's birth father. Bruce didn't know what to think, and told him to leave.

But later, Bruce stared in the mirror, haunted by strange imaginings.

Thirty years earlier, as a military scientist, David Banner had performed secret experiments that had changed his own genes. When Bruce was born, the genes passed from father to son. Now Bruce seemed to have super strong cells. They could withstand energy that would kill other people.

David Banner wanted to know more. As the night janitor at Bruce's lab, he was keeping an eye on Bruce . . . and stealing Bruce and Betty's research!

Back in his lab, Bruce tested his blood to see what was happening inside his body. Why was he so different? Was his life spinning out of control? He began to shake. He could feel his anger rising . . . taking over. He couldn't stop it.

In seconds, Bruce's skin turned green. His body grew to twice its normal size. His muscles bulged, tearing his clothes. Now his strength was superhuman!

He was the Hulk!

In his rage, the Hulk destroyed everything in sight.

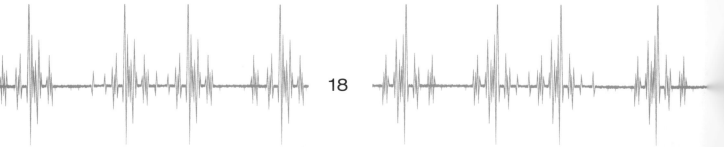

David Banner saw it all—and realized that the gammasphere accident had changed his son. Bruce's strong cells, plus gamma radiation, plus anger equals the Hulk!

The next morning, Betty visited Bruce's house. The place was a mess. So was Bruce. He told her about meeting his father, but he couldn't remember anything after that.

"Betty, what's happening to me?" asked Bruce.

That's when Betty's father, General Ross, came to the door with the military police. They had found Bruce's torn clothing and his wallet in the wrecked lab.

Ross told the troop to keep Bruce under house arrest.

He told Betty to stay away from Bruce.

Betty went looking for answers. She tracked down David Banner, but he wasn't very helpful.

"Bruce has made it clear he wants nothing to do with me," David Banner said. "Now, if you'll excuse me, Miss Ross, I have some work to do."

If only Betty had known what kind of work . . .

Later, Bruce received a disturbing phone call from his father, hinting that he was going to hurt Betty. Bruce had to help her. But how? He was a prisoner in his own home. Then Talbot showed up. He picked a fight and threatened a hostile takeover of Bruce's lab.

It was all too much. "You're making me angry," Bruce warned Talbot. "I don't think you'd like me when I'm angry."

But Talbot didn't back off. Soon he met the Hulk face to face!

Smashing out of the house, the Hulk went looking for Betty. He had to protect her. He found her at her cabin in the woods.

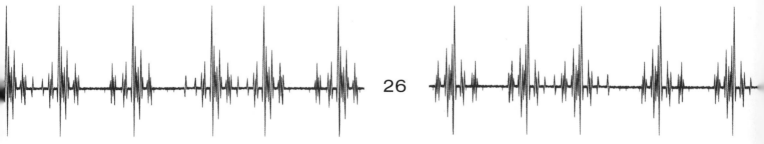

"Hello?" Betty called out, after hearing a noise outside.

When she saw the Hulk, Betty could not believe her eyes.

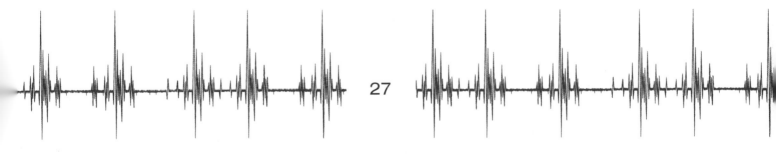

The Hulk had arrived just in time. From out of the woods jumped three vicious Hulk-Dogs sent by David Banner! He had used the stolen research from the lab, and turned ordinary dogs into monsters. Then he had sent them to attack Betty.

Luckily, the mutated dogs were no match
for the Hulk. One by one, he destroyed them
while Betty took shelter inside her car.

When the danger was over, the Hulk calmed
down . . . and became Bruce again.

Betty was so worried about Bruce, she called her father for help.

"I didn't know what else to do," Betty explained to Bruce, as a team of soldiers swooped down on the cabin. General Ross had sent them to get Bruce and take him to a military base in the desert.

There, Betty hoped they could study Bruce and help him.

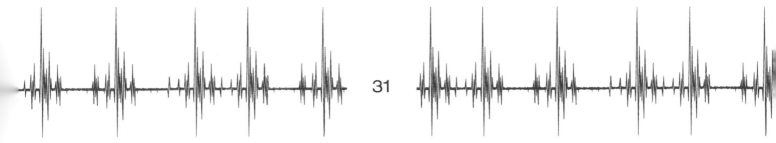

Bruce soon found out that he had grown up on this military compound. It was called Desert Base. Parts of it looked familiar, but he had no clear memories of living in the now abandoned neighborhood.

"I bet *it* remembers," said Bruce, referring to the monster inside of him. "I feel him now, watching me, hating me."

Bruce and Betty returned to the Desert Base lab to find that Talbot had been put in charge of studying Bruce.

Talbot ordered Betty off the base. Then he came at Bruce with an electric prod.

"I need your cells to trigger some chemical distress signals," Talbot explained. "You know, so you can get a little green for me again."

Talbot wanted a sample of the Hulk's cells to analyze. He planned to copy them, and sell them for profit.

When the prod didn't work, Talbot forced Bruce into an immersion tank. He hooked Bruce up to machines that triggered his brain waves. Soon Bruce was reliving forgotten and painful memories from his childhood.

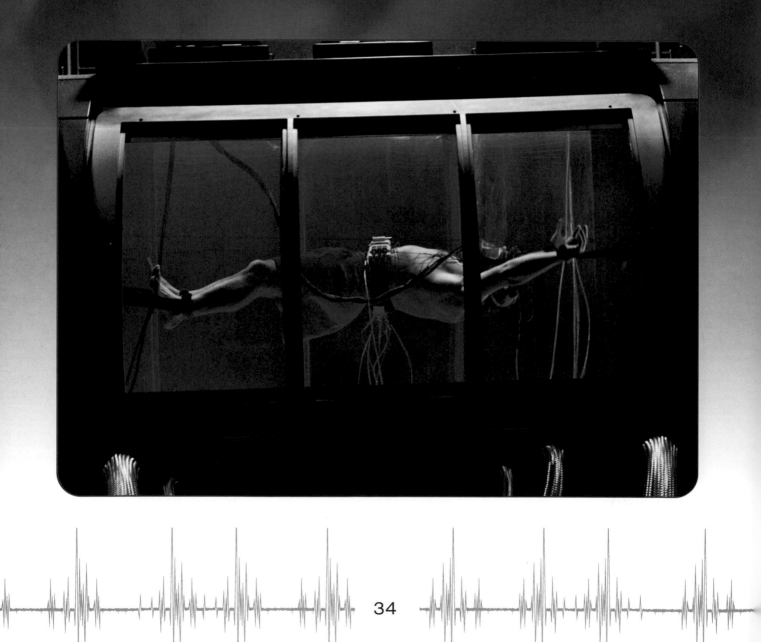

Inside Bruce's body, the pent-up stress and anger were triggering a change.

Talbot had asked for it, and he got it: the Hulk.

The Hulk smashed his way out of the immersion tank. Talbot and the Atheon security guards were powerless against him. General Ross tried to take control. But even his troops could not stop the Hulk. Bullets barely scratched him. He muscled his way up and out of the underground lab.

Before long, the Hulk was racing off into the desert, heading west toward San Francisco. General Ross boarded a helicopter and chased after him.

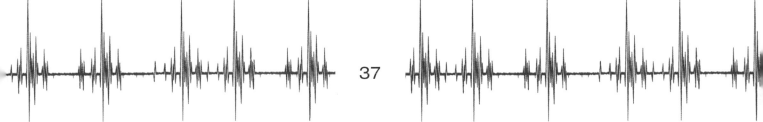

"Oh, no," said General Ross, astonished by the Hulk's amazing speed. He watched in awe as the Hulk bounded through the air, covering miles in seconds with one fantastic leap after another.

The Hulk raced past the army tanks—their weapons could not stop him.

Three F-22 fighter jets caught up with the Hulk over the Sierra Nevada mountains. They followed him west to San Francisco, where the Hulk jumped onto one of the arches of the Golden Gate Bridge.

As one of the jets whizzed by him, the Hulk jumped onto it. On orders from General Ross, the pilot flew the jet straight up, rocketing into the clouds. The Hulk hung on—until he passed out from lack of oxygen. He fell, landing with a tremendous splash in the San Francisco Bay.

The Hulk wasn't defeated yet. He awoke underwater, and spied some drains flowing into the bay. He forced his huge body into one of them.

Now the Hulk was under the city. Streets cracked, water mains broke, and fire hydrants exploded as he stormed through the sewer system.

The Hulk burst through a manhole cover and climbed up onto the street.

He was not alone. Waiting for him were a fleet of helicopters, the National Guard, SWAT teams, and hundreds of police officers.

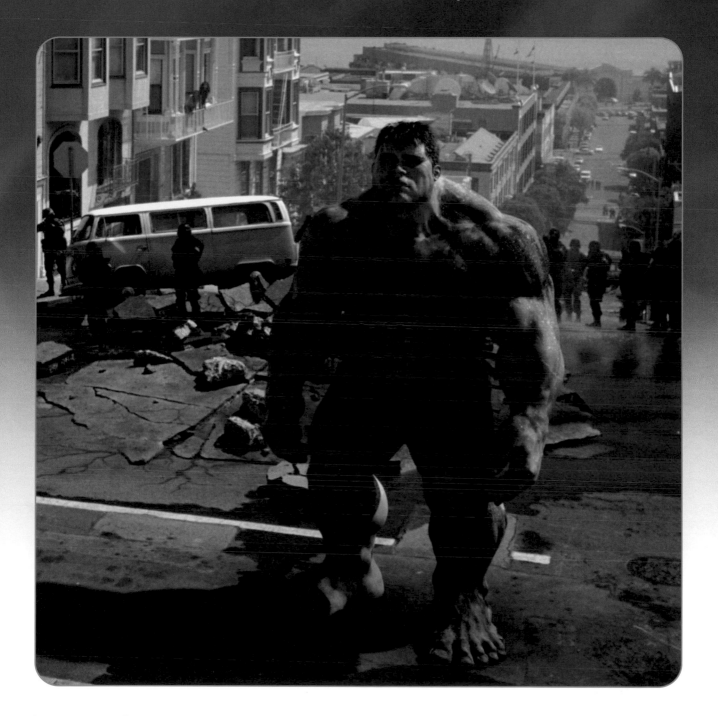

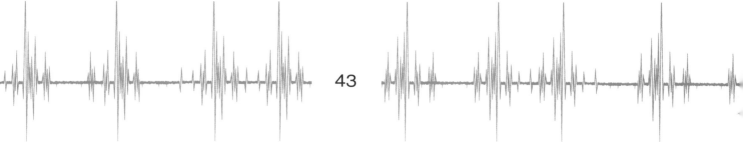

Meanwhile, General Ross had found Betty and picked her up in his helicopter.

"Betty," he said, "I don't know what choice I have. I must destroy him."

"You can't," Betty replied. "Enraging him just makes him stronger." She had a better idea: calm the Hulk down.

"All units, hold your fire," General Ross commanded.

In the midst of the standoff, Ross landed the chopper and Betty emerged. Spotting her, the Hulk dropped to his knees, crying out in shame. The instant she touched him, his body began to shrink. Fluids oozed out of every pore, and within seconds, it was Bruce—not the Hulk—standing before Betty.

The beast was gone, but for how long?

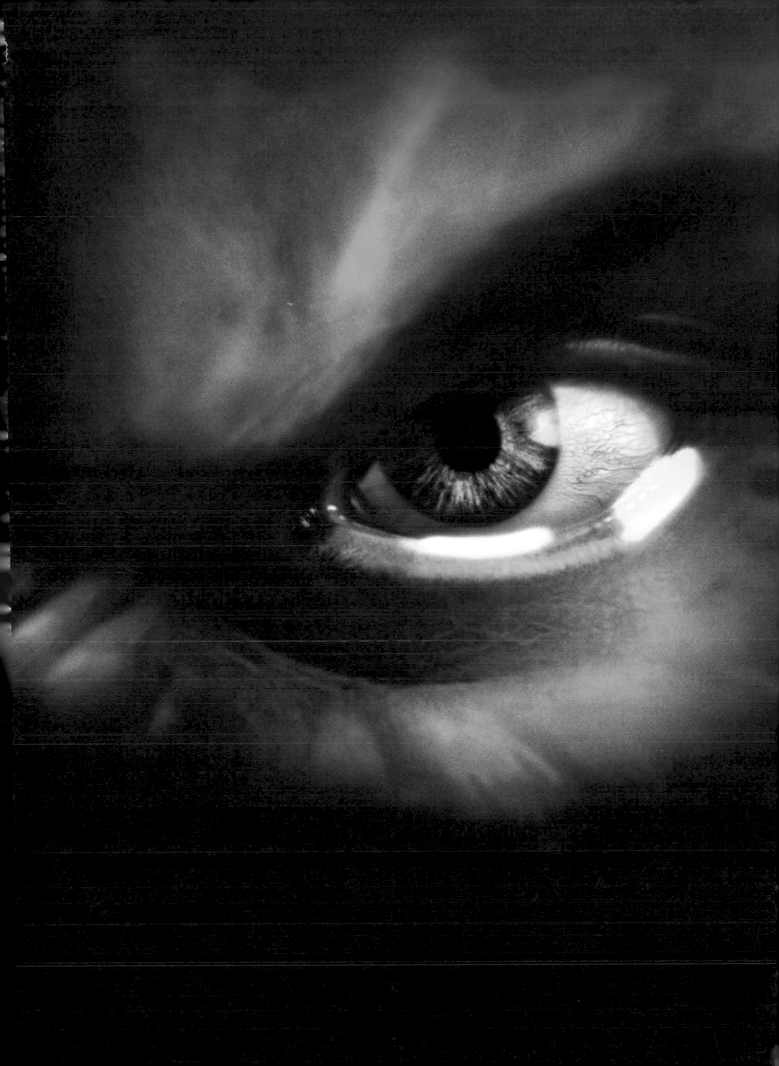